Alice's Adventures in Wonderland

Lewis Carroll

Condensed and Adapted by
DEBBIE GUTHERY

Illustrated by
JASON ALEXANDER

Cover Illustrated by
PATRICK WHELAN

Dalmatian Press

The Junior Classics have been
adapted and illustrated with care and thought
to introduce you to a world of famous authors, characters, ideas,
and great stories that have been loved for generations.

Editor — Kathryn Knight
Creative Director — Gina Rhodes-Haynes
And the entire classics project team
of Dalmatian Publishing Group

A note to the reader—

A classic story rests in your hands. The characters are famous. The tale is timeless.

This Junior Classic edition of *Alice's Adventures in Wonderland* has been carefully condensed and adapted from the original version (which you really *must* read when you're ready for every detail). We kept the well-known phrases for you. We kept Lewis Carroll's style. And we kept the important imagery and heart of the tale.

Literature is terrific fun! It encourages you to think. It helps you dream. It is full of heroes and villains, suspense and humor, adventure and wonder, and new ideas. It introduces you to writers who reach out across time to say: "Do you want to hear a story I wrote?"

Curl up and enjoy.

CONTENTS

CHARACTERS

ALICE — a young girl with a mind of her own (in a world not her own)

ALICE'S SISTER — an older, sensible young lady who is reading to Alice

DINAH — Alice's cat

THE WHITE RABBIT — a well-dressed rabbit who is running a bit late

THE MOUSE — a new friend in the pool of tears who would rather not hear of cats

DUCK, DODO, LORY, EAGLET, CRAB, MAGPIE, CANARY — animals caught in the pool of tears

BILL — a poor fellow who is sent down–and kicked out of–a chimney

THE CATERPILLAR — a three-inch mushroom-sitter who gives advice

FISH-FOOTMAN — a footman for the Queen

FROG-FOOTMAN — a footman for the Duchess

THE DUCHESS — a rather rude woman who is fond of morals

THE CHESHIRE CAT — the Duchess's grinning cat who tends to disappear

CHARACTERS

THE COOK — the Duchess's cook who makes pepper soup

THE MARCH HARE — the host of a tea party outside his house

THE MAD HATTER — an odd tea party guest who does not do well with keeping Time

DORMOUSE — a sleepy guest at the tea party

TWO, SEVEN AND FIVE — three royal gardeners who are truly cards

THE QUEEN OF HEARTS — the ruler of the croquet game (and everyone's head)

THE KING OF HEARTS — the Queen's patient and rather dull husband

THE KNAVE OF HEARTS — a royal servant who may have stolen some tarts

THE GRYPHON — a droll creature who introduces Alice to the Mock Turtle

THE MOCK TURTLE — a very sad and tearful teller of tales

Alice's Adventures in Wonderland

CHAPTER ONE

Down the Rabbit Hole

Alice was beginning to get tired of sitting by her sister on the riverbank with nothing to do. Once or twice she had peered into the book her sister was reading, but it had no pictures or conversations in it, "and what good is a book," thought Alice, "without pictures or conversations?"

She thought about making a daisy chain but didn't feel like getting up and picking the daisies, so she laid her head in her sister's lap and watched the clouds. Suddenly a White Rabbit with pink eyes ran by.

"Oh, dear! Oh, dear! I will be late!" the Rabbit said.

It took a watch out of its pocket, looked at it, and then hurried away.

Being very curious, Alice jumped to her feet and ran across the field after it. She was just in time to see it pop down a large rabbit hole under the hedge. Without thinking, she followed.

The rabbit hole was a long tunnel that seemed to go on forever. She made her way through the narrow passageway as best she could, when suddenly it dropped down. Alice didn't have a minute to think before she realized she was falling down a very deep well.

She seemed to be falling very slowly, so she spent her time looking around. Cupboards, bookshelves, maps, and pictures that hung upon nails filled the walls of the well. She took down a jar from one of the shelves as she passed it. It was labeled "ORANGE MARMALADE," but to her disappointment it was empty, so she carefully put it back into one of the cupboards as she fell past it.

Down, down, down she went. Would the fall ever come to an end? "I wonder how many miles I've fallen?" she said out loud. "I must be getting near the center of the earth. I wonder if I will fall right *through* it!"

ALICE'S ADVENTURES IN WONDERLAND

Down, down, down. There was nothing else to do, so Alice began talking to herself.

"Dinah will miss me, I think!" (Dinah was her cat.) "Oh, I wish you were down here with me, Dinah!" She dozed off and dreamed that she was walking hand in hand with her cat, when suddenly, thump! thump! down she came upon a heap of sticks and dry leaves, and the fall was over.

Alice stood up and wiped herself off. She looked up to see where she had fallen from, but it was too dark to see anything at all. In front of her was another long passageway, and the White Rabbit was hurrying down it. There wasn't a moment to lose. Away she went after the Rabbit. "Oh, my ears and whiskers, how late it's getting!" she heard it say. She ran like the wind to catch up to it, but the Rabbit was gone.

There she stood, alone in a long hallway that was lit up by a row of lamps hanging from the ceiling. There were doors all around the hall, but they were all locked. She began to wonder if she was ever going to get out again. She decided to walk a little farther ahead to see what she could find.

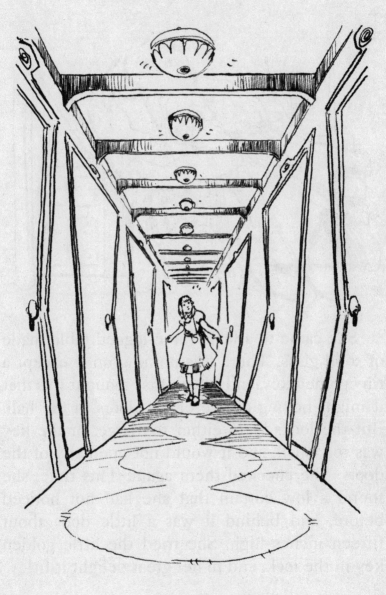

She came to a little three-legged table made of solid glass. There was nothing on it except a tiny golden key, and Alice's first thought was that it might belong to one of the doors in the hall. But the locks were either too large, or the key was too small, and it would not open any of the doors. She checked them again. This time, she found a low curtain that she had not noticed before, and behind it was a little door about fifteen inches high. She tried the little golden key in the lock, and to her great delight it fit!

Alice opened the door. She knelt down to look through it and saw the most beautiful garden she had ever seen. How she wished to get out of that dark hall and wander around the beds of bright flowers and cool fountains, but she could not even get her head through the doorway.

She went back to the table, hoping she would find another key on it, or perhaps a book of rules to tell her how to get through the door. This time she found a little bottle on it (that was not there before). Around the neck of the bottle was a paper label, with the words "DRINK ME" printed on it in large letters.

Alice picked up the bottle and, seeing that it was not marked "Poison," she tasted it. It was delicious, and she quickly finished it.

"What a curious feeling!" said Alice. "I must be getting smaller."

She was right. She was now only ten inches high. "Now I am the right size to go through the little door and into that beautiful garden," she thought to herself. Alice went back to the door, but had forgotten the little golden key. When she went back to the table for it, she could not reach it.

She could see it through the glass, and she tried her best to climb up one of the legs of the table, but it was too slippery. Alice sat down and cried. As she wiped the tears from her eyes, she noticed a little glass box lying under the table.

She opened it and found a small cake that had the words "EAT ME" marked out in raisins. "Well, I'll eat it," said Alice, "and if it makes me grow bigger, I can reach the key. If it makes me grow smaller, I can slide under the door. Either way I'll get into the garden, and I don't care which happens!"

She ate a little bit, and held her hand on the top of her head to feel which way it was growing. She was surprised to find that she remained the same size, so she set to work, and soon finished off the cake.

CHAPTER TWO

The Pool of Tears

"Curiouser and curiouser!" cried Alice. "I'm growing like a garden weed! Good-bye, feet!" In fact she had sprouted up to over nine feet high. She grabbed the little golden key off the table and hurried back to the garden door.

Poor Alice! Now she was too big to fit through the door and all she could do was lie down on one side and look through into the garden with one eye. She sat up and began to cry again.

"You ought to be ashamed of yourself," she said, "crying like this! Stop it right now!" But she went on, shedding gallons of tears, until there was a large pool around her, about four inches deep and reaching halfway down the hall.

She heard a little pattering of feet in the distance, and she quickly dried her eyes to see what was coming. It was the White Rabbit, all dressed up, with a pair of white gloves in one hand and a large fan in the other. He was in a great hurry and muttering to himself, "Oh, the Duchess, the Duchess! Oh! She will be angry if I keep her waiting!"

Alice was desperate for help, so she decided to see if the Rabbit might have some ideas. She said in a timid voice, "If you please, sir—"

The Rabbit was startled. He dropped the white gloves and the fan, and scurried away into the darkness as fast as he could go. "Oh, now what am I going to do?" she sighed.

Alice put the key on the table and picked up the fan and gloves. Since the hall was very hot, she fanned herself. "Who in the world am I?" she said. "I'm sure I'm not Ada, or Mabel. Oh, my. Do I still remember all my school lessons?" (Then she practiced her math and geography—which all came out wrong!) "Everything is so different and *I* am so different," she said, very confused.

As she was talking, she looked down and saw that she had put on one of the little gloves. "Wait!" she said. "How did I put on this glove? I must be growing small again, but how?" She had been cooling herself with the Rabbit's fan. Suddenly she realized the fanning was making her grow smaller and smaller. She dropped the fan, just in time.

"That was close!" said Alice, frightened at the sudden change, but very glad to find she was still in one piece. "Oh, the garden!" She ran as fast as she could back to the little door, but the little door was shut again and the little golden key was lying on the glass table just like before.

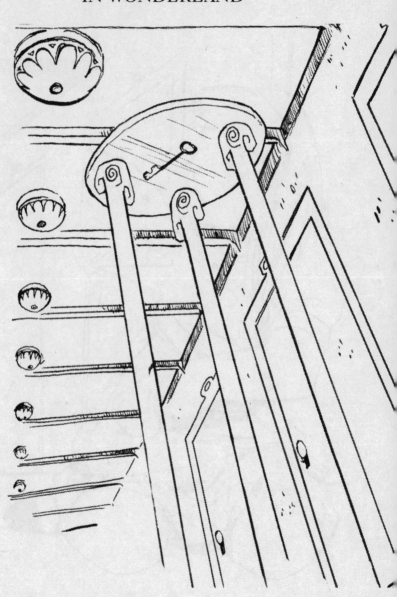

Suddenly she slipped. Splash! There she was up to her chin in saltwater. She had fallen into the pool of tears, which she had cried when she was nine feet high.

"I wish I hadn't cried so much!" said Alice, as she swam around, trying to find a way out. "I hope I don't drown in my own tears!"

Just then she heard something splashing around in the pool and she swam toward it. At first she thought it must be a walrus or hippopotamus, but then she remembered how small she was and saw that it was only a mouse.

"I wonder if I can speak to this mouse? There's no harm in trying," thought Alice, so she said, "O Mouse, do you know a way out of this pool?" The Mouse looked at her and seemed to her to wink with one of its little eyes, but it said nothing.

"Perhaps it doesn't understand English," thought Alice. "Maybe it's a French mouse." So she said, *"Où est ma chatte?"* (which means: "Where is my cat?"). The Mouse jumped out of the water and fell back in, shaking with fright. "Oh, I am so sorry!" cried Alice. "I forgot that you don't like cats."

"Not like cats!" cried the Mouse. "Would *you* like cats if you were me?" The Mouse was trembling down to the end of its tail.

"Oh, I'm so sorry to have frightened you," said Alice. "Please don't swim away."

"Let's get to the shore," replied the Mouse, "and then I'll tell you why I hate cats."

By this time, the pool was getting crowded with the birds and animals that had fallen into it. There was a Duck and a Dodo, a Lory and an Eaglet, and several other strange creatures. Alice led the way, and the creatures followed her to shore.

CHAPTER THREE

A Caucus Race and a Long Tale

They were a strange-looking group of wet creatures. The birds' feathers were drenched and the animals' fur was clinging to them.

The first question of course was, *How to get dry?* They all talked this over, and Alice joined in as if she had known them all her life.

At last the Dodo rose solemnly to his feet and said, "I move that the meeting be over, for the immediate adoption of an energetic remedy—"

"Speak English!" said the Eaglet. "I don't understand anything you just said, and I don't think you do either!" The Eaglet bent down its head to hide a smile.

"What I was going to say," said the Dodo, "was that the best thing to get us dry would be a Caucus Race."

"What is a Caucus Race?" said Alice.

"Why," said the Dodo, "the best way to explain it is to do it."

The Dodo marked out a race course. It was a sort of circle, and then everyone was placed along the course here and there. There was no "One, two, three, go!" but everyone began running when they liked, and stopped when they liked, so that it was not easy to know when the race was over. However, when they had been running half an hour or so, and were quite dry again, the Dodo suddenly called out, "The race is over!" and they all crowded around it, panting, and asking, "Who has won?"

The Dodo thought and declared, "Everybody has won, and everyone must have prizes."

"But who is going to give the prizes?" a chorus of voices asked.

"Why, *she* is, of course," said the Dodo, pointing to Alice with one finger.

The whole party crowded around her, calling out, "Prizes! Prizes!"

Alice had no idea what to do, and in despair she put her hand in her pocket and pulled out a box of candies (which had stayed nicely dry). She handed them round as prizes. There was exactly one for each of them.

"But she must have a prize herself, you know," said the Mouse.

"Of course," the Dodo replied. "What else have you got in your pocket?" it went on, turning to Alice.

"Only a thimble," said Alice sadly.

"Hand it over here," said the Dodo.

Then they all crowded around her once more, while the Dodo presented the thimble, saying, "We beg you to accept this thimble." When it had finished the speech, they all cheered.

Alice thought the whole thing very strange, but she bowed, and took the thimble, looking as serious as she could.

Then they sat down in a circle, and begged the Mouse to tell them a story.

"You promised to tell me your story, you know," said Alice, "about why you hate—C's," she said in a whisper, afraid that she would upset him again.

"Mine is a long and sad tale!" said the Mouse, turning to Alice, and sighing.

Alice looked at the mouse's tail. "It *is* a long tail," said Alice, "but why do you call it sad?" And she kept wondering about it while the Mouse was speaking, and this is what she saw in her mind while the Mouse told its story—

ALICE'S ADVENTURES
IN WONDERLAND

Furry said to
a mouse, That
he met in the
house, "Let
us both go
to the law.
I will prose-
cute *you*.—
Come, I'll
take no
denial. We
must have
a trial.
For really
this morn-
ing I've
nothing
to do."
Said the
mouse to
the cat,
"Such a
trial, as
that, With
no jury
or judge,
would
be wast-
ing our
breath."
"I'll be
judge,
I'll be
jury,"
Purred
cunning
old Furry,
"I'll try
the
whole
case,
and
put
you to
death."

"You are not listening!" said the Mouse to Alice angrily. "What are you thinking of?"

"I beg your pardon," said Alice very humbly. "You had gotten to the fifth curve of your tail, I think?"

"I had *not!*" cried the Mouse, angrily.

"A knot!" said Alice, "Oh, do let me help to undo it!"

"I shall do nothing of the sort," said the Mouse, getting up and walking away. "You have insulted me by talking such nonsense!"

"I didn't mean it!" said Alice.

The Mouse only growled in reply.

"Please come back and finish your story!" Alice called out to it, and all the others joined in chorus, "Yes, please do!" but the Mouse only shook its head and walked away quickly.

"What a pity!" said the Lory.

An old Crab said to her daughter, "Let this be a lesson to you never to lose your temper!"

"Hold your tongue, Ma!" said the young Crab, a little snappishly. "You're enough to try the patience of an oyster!"

"I wish I had Dinah here!" said Alice aloud, to nobody in particular. "She would bring the Mouse back!"

"And who is Dinah, if I might ask?" said the Lory.

Alice replied eagerly, "Dinah's my cat. She's very good at catching mice! And, oh! You should

see her catch birds! Why, she'll eat a little bird as soon as she looks at it!"

This made the creatures uncomfortable. Some of the birds flew away immediately. An old Magpie quickly gathered itself up and said, "I really must be getting home," and a Canary called out in a trembling voice to its children, "Come away, my dears. It's time you were all in bed!" Alice was soon left alone.

"I wish I hadn't mentioned Dinah! Nobody seems to like her down here! I wonder if I will ever see her any more!" Alice began to cry again, for she felt lonely. In a while, she heard a little pattering of footsteps. She looked up eagerly, hoping that the Mouse had changed his mind and was coming back to finish his story.

CHAPTER FOUR

The Rabbit Sends in a Little Bill

It was the White Rabbit, looking around as it came toward her. She heard it muttering to itself, "The Duchess! The Duchess! Oh, my dear paws! Oh, my fur and whiskers! She'll have me executed. Where could I have dropped them?" Alice knew it was looking for the fan and the pair of white gloves, and she began hunting for them, but they were nowhere to be found.

The Rabbit noticed Alice and called out to her in an angry tone, "Why, Mary Ann, what are you doing out here? Run home this moment, and fetch me a pair of gloves and a fan! Quick, now!" Alice was so frightened that she ran off in the direction it pointed to, without trying to explain that she was not Mary Ann.

She came to a neat little house and on the door was a bright brass plate with the name "W. RABBIT" engraved on it. She went in without knocking, and hurried upstairs, in great fear that she should meet the real Mary Ann, who might tell her to leave before Alice had found the fan and gloves.

"How strange it is," Alice said to herself, "to be taking orders from a rabbit!"

She found a little room with a table by the window, and on it were a fan and two or three pairs of tiny white gloves. She picked up the fan and a pair of the gloves, and was going to leave the room, when her eye spied a bottle near the mirror. There was no label this time with the words "DRINK ME," but she uncorked it and put it to her lips. "I know something will happen. I do hope it'll make me grow big again. I'm tired of being little!"

She grew sooner than she had expected. Before she had drunk half the bottle, her head was pressing against the ceiling. She quickly put down the bottle and said, "I hope I won't grow any more."

It was too late to wish that! She went on growing and growing and soon she had to kneel down on the floor. When she was too big for *that*,

ALICE'S ADVENTURES
IN WONDERLAND

she tried lying down with one elbow against the door, and the other arm curled round her head. On and on she grew. She put one arm out the window, and one foot up the chimney—and that was all the room she had. "What will happen to me?" she said.

Luckily for Alice, the little magic bottle had now had its full effect, and she quit growing. She was very uncomfortable, and it seemed that she would not be going anywhere for a while.

After a few minutes had passed, she heard a voice outside. "Mary Ann! Mary Ann!" said the voice. "Fetch me my gloves this moment!" Then came a little pattering of feet on the stairs. Alice knew it was the Rabbit coming to look for her.

The Rabbit came to the door and tried to open it, but the door opened inward, and Alice's elbow was pressed hard against it. Alice heard it say, "Then I'll go around to the window and climb in that way."

"No, you won't," thought Alice. When she heard the Rabbit outside the window, she spread out her hand and made a grab at the air. She did not get hold of anything, but she heard a little shriek, a fall, and a crash of broken glass.

Next she heard the Rabbit's angry voice— "Pat! Pat! Where are you?" And then she heard a voice that she had never heard before: "I'm here! Digging for apples, yer Honor!"

"Digging for apples, indeed!" said the Rabbit angrily. "Come here! And help me out of this!"

(There were sounds of more broken glass.)

"Now, Pat, what do you see in that window?"

"An arm, yer Honor!"

"An arm? You goose! Whoever saw one that size? Why, it fills the whole window!"

"Sure, it does, yer Honor—but it's an arm, all the same."

"Well, it's got no business there. Go and take it away!"

There was a long silence after this, and Alice could only hear whispers.

Then she went for a while without hearing anything else. Suddenly there was a rumbling of a cart's wheels and the sound of many voices all talking at once. "Where's the other ladder?— Why, I didn't bring but one—Bill's got the other—Bill! Fetch it here, lad!—Here, put 'em up at this corner—No, tie 'em together first— They don't reach high enough yet—Oh! They are fine. Don't be particular—Here, Bill! Catch this rope—Will the roof hold?—Watch out for that loose slate—Oh, it's coming down! Heads below!"—(A loud crash)—"Now, who did that?—It was Bill—Who's to go down the chimney?—Not, I! You do it!—I won't!—Bill must go down—Here, Bill! The master says you need to go down the chimney!"

"Oh! So Bill gets to come down the chimney, does he?" said Alice to herself. "They seem to make Bill do everything! I wouldn't be in Bill's place for anything! This fireplace is narrow, but I think I can kick a little!"

She pulled her foot back as far as she could and waited until she heard a little animal scratching and scrambling in the chimney close above her. She said to herself, "This is Bill," and gave one sharp kick—then waited to see what would happen next.

She heard everyone shout, "There goes Bill!" The Rabbit's voice screamed, "Catch him, you by the hedge!" Then there was silence, and then more voices—"Hold up his head—Don't choke him—How are you, old fellow?—Tell us all about it!"

She heard a very soft voice say, "Well, I hardly

ALICE'S ADVENTURES
IN WONDERLAND

know—but I'm too worn out to tell you everything. All I know is that something came at me like a Jack-in-the-box, and up I went like a skyrocket!"

"So you did, old fellow!" said the others.

"We must burn the house down!" said the Rabbit's voice.

Alice called out as loud as she could, "If you do, I'll send Dinah after you!"

There was a long silence.

Alice thought to herself, "I wonder what they will do next."

After a minute or two, they began moving around again, and Alice heard the Rabbit say, "A wheelbarrow full will be enough."

"A barrow full of what?" thought Alice. She didn't have long to think, when a shower of little pebbles came rattling through the window. Some of them hit her in the face. "I'll put a stop to this," she said to herself. She shouted out, "You'd better not do that again!"

There was another long silence.

Alice noticed that the pebbles were all turning into little cakes as they lay on the floor. This gave Alice an idea. "If I eat one of these

cakes," she thought, "it's sure to make some change in my size. It can't possibly make me larger so it must make me smaller."

So she swallowed one of the cakes—

—and was delighted to find that she began shrinking. As soon as she was small enough to get through the door, she ran out of the house and found a crowd of little animals and birds waiting outside. They all made a rush at Alice, but she ran away as fast as she could. She soon found herself safe in some thick woods.

Alice thought, "The first thing I need to do is to grow to my right size again and then I will find a way back to the beautiful garden."

It sounded like good plan, but she didn't have the slightest idea how she would do it.

There was a large mushroom growing near her. It was just her height. She looked all around it and decided to see what was on the top of it.

She stretched herself up on tiptoe and peered over the edge of the mushroom. Her eyes met the eyes of a large, blue caterpillar that was sitting on the top with its arms folded, quietly smoking a long pipe.

CHAPTER FIVE

Advice from a Caterpillar

The Caterpillar and Alice looked at each other for some time in silence. At last the Caterpillar took the pipe out of its mouth and spoke to her in a sleepy voice.

"Who are *you*?" he asked.

Alice replied, "I—I don't know, sir—at least I knew who I was when I got up this morning, but I have changed so many sizes since then."

"What do you mean by that?" said the Caterpillar sternly. "Explain yourself!"

"I can't explain *myself*," said Alice, "because I'm not myself, you see."

"I don't see," said the Caterpillar.

"I can't put it more clearly," Alice replied politely. "I can't understand it myself to begin with. I have been so many sizes today—it is very confusing."

"It isn't," said the Caterpillar.

"Well, maybe not to *you*," said Alice, "but when you have to turn into a chrysalis and then after that into a butterfly, I think you'll feel a little strange, won't you?"

"Not a bit," said the Caterpillar.

"Well, maybe your feelings will change," said Alice. "It has been very strange to me."

"You!" said the Caterpillar. "Who are *you*?"

She replied, "I think you ought to tell me who *you* are, first."

"Why?" said the Caterpillar.

He had a good point and didn't seem to be in a good mood, so she decided to leave and began walking away.

"Come back!" the Caterpillar called after her. "I've something important to say!"

Alice turned and came back again.

"Keep your temper," said the Caterpillar.

"Is that all?" said Alice, holding in her anger as well as she could.

"No," said the Caterpillar.

Alice thought she might as well wait. The Caterpillar might tell her something worth hearing. For some minutes it puffed away without speaking, but at last it unfolded its arms, took the pipe out of its mouth again, and said, "So you think you're changed, do you?"

"I'm afraid I am, sir," said Alice. "I don't stay the same size for longer than ten minutes!"

"What size do you want to be?" it asked.

"Oh, I really don't care what size I am," Alice replied. "I just don't like changing sizes so much—do you know what I mean?"

"I *don't* know," said the Caterpillar.

Alice said nothing. She felt that she was losing her temper again.

"Are you happy with your size now?" said the Caterpillar.

"Well, I would like to be a *little* larger, if you wouldn't mind," said Alice. "Three inches is such a terrible height to be."

"It is a very *good* height indeed!" said the Caterpillar angrily, rearing itself upright as it spoke. (It was exactly three inches high.)

"But I'm not used to it!" pleaded poor Alice.

"You'll get used to it in time," said the Caterpillar. It put the pipe back into its mouth and began smoking again.

This time Alice waited until the Caterpillar chose to speak again. The Caterpillar took the pipe out of its mouth and yawned once or twice, and then shook itself. Then it got down off the mushroom and crawled away in the grass, saying as it went, "One side will make you grow taller, and the other side will make you grow shorter."

"One side of *what*? The other side of *what*?" said Alice.

"Of the mushroom," said the Caterpillar and then it crawled out of sight.

Alice looked at the mushroom, trying to figure out which two sides did what. It was perfectly round, so it was hard to choose. She stretched her arms around it as far as they would go, and broke off a bit of the edge with each hand.

"And now which is which?" she said to herself, and nibbled a little of the right-hand bit to see what would happen. The next moment—

—she felt a blow underneath her chin! It had struck her foot!

The sudden change frightened her, but she had to hurry. She was shrinking fast. She quickly took a bite of the other bit. Her chin was pressed so hard against her foot there was hardly enough room to open her mouth. She managed to swallow a small bit of the left-hand side of the mushroom.

"My head is free at last!" Alice said with delight. Her happiness faded when she realized she could not see her shoulders. All she could see was her long neck, which seemed to poke out above some green leaves that lay far below her.

"What *can* all that green stuff be?" said Alice. "And where *have* my shoulders gone? And, oh, my poor hands, why can't I see you?" She was moving them about but she saw no result, except a little shaking in the green leaves.

She couldn't get her hands to her head so she tried to get her head to her hands. Her neck bent in any direction, like a snake. She started curving it down into the leaves, which she found out were the tops of trees.

Alice moved her neck in and out of the trees. It kept getting tangled among the branches, so she had to stop and untwist it until, at last, she found her shoulders. She remembered that she still held the pieces of mushroom in her hands, and started nibbling at one and then at the other. She grew sometimes taller and sometimes smaller, until she finally got back to her regular height.

It had been such a long time since she had been the right size that it felt strange at first, but she got used to it in a few minutes.

"There's half my plan done now! I'm back to my right size, and now I'm off to find that beautiful garden—but how *do* I find it?" As she said this, she saw in front of her a little house about four feet high.

"I can't go to that house being *this* size. I would scare whoever lives there out of their wits!" So she began eating the right-hand bit of mushroom again, and didn't go near the house until she was nine inches high.

CHAPTER SIX

Pig and Pepper

She stood looking at the house, when suddenly a footman came running out of the woods. Alice thought he looked like a fish. He knocked on the door with his knuckles. It was opened by another footman in uniform with a round face and large eyes like a frog.

The Fish Footman handed a letter over to the other saying, "For the Duchess. An invitation from the Queen to play croquet." The Frog Footman answered, "From the Queen. An invitation for the Duchess to play croquet."

Then they both bowed low, and their curls tangled together.

Alice laughed so much at this that she had to run back into the woods for fear of their hearing her. When she peeped out, the Fish Footman was gone, and the other was sitting on the ground near the door. He was staring up into the sky.

Alice went up to the door and knocked.

"There's no use in knocking," said the Footman, "because I'm on the same side of the door as you are and they're making so much noise inside, no one could possibly hear you."

The noises coming from inside *were* very loud. There was a constant howling and sneezing, and every now and then a great crash, as if a dish or kettle had been broken to pieces.

"Please, then," said Alice, "how am I to get in?"

"I shall sit here," the Footman remarked, paying no attention to Alice, "till tomorrow—"

The door of the house opened, and a large plate came flying out, straight at the Footman's head. It almost hit his nose. It broke into a million pieces against one of the trees behind him.

"—or next day, maybe," the Footman continued, as if nothing had happened.

"Oh, there's no use talking to him," said Alice, and she opened the door and went in.

The door led right into a large kitchen, which was full of smoke. The Duchess was sitting on a three-legged stool, holding a baby. The cook was leaning over the fire stirring a large pot which seemed to be full of soup.

"There's too much pepper in that soup!" Alice said to herself, as she sneezed.

Even the Duchess sneezed occasionally. As for the baby, it was sneezing and howling. The only creatures in the kitchen that did *not* sneeze were the cook and a large cat which was sitting near the fireplace, grinning from ear to ear.

"Please can you tell me," said Alice, "why your cat grins like that?"

"It's a Cheshire cat," said the Duchess, "and that's why."

"I didn't know that Cheshire cats always grinned. In fact, I didn't know that cats *could* grin."

"They all can," said the Duchess, "and most of 'em do."

"I don't know of any that do," Alice said very politely.

"You don't know much," said the Duchess.

Alice did not at all like what the Duchess said, and decided she better change the subject. Suddenly the cook took the pot of soup off the fire, and at once started throwing everything within her reach at the Duchess and the baby. The Duchess didn't seem to notice, even when a plate hit her. The baby was crying so much already that it was impossible to know if it was hurt or not.

"Oh, *please* be careful with what you're doing!" cried Alice, jumping up.

"If everybody minded their own business," the Duchess said, "the world would go around a great deal faster."

"Which would not be very good at all," said Alice, who was showing off a little of her knowledge. "Just think what a mess that would make, having shorter days and nights! You see, the Earth takes twenty-four hours to turn around on its axis—"

"Oh, don't bother me," said the Duchess. "I never did like mathematics!" And she began rocking her child again, singing a sort of lullaby to it, giving it a bounce at the end of every line.

The Duchess sang the second verse of the song, and then turned to Alice.

"Here! You may hold it a bit if you like!" the Duchess, tossing the baby to her as she spoke. "I must go and get ready to play croquet with the Queen," and she hurried out of the room. The cook threw a frying pan after her as she went out, but it just missed her.

Alice caught the baby with some difficulty. Its arms and legs went in all directions. The poor little thing was snorting like a steam engine when she caught it, and kept curling and uncurling itself out again. Soon she was able to properly hold it and she carried it outside. "If I don't take this child away," thought Alice, "they're sure to hurt it." She said the words out loud, and the little thing grunted in reply. "Don't grunt," said Alice. "It's not good manners."

The baby grunted again, and Alice looked into its face to see what was the matter with it. It had a *very* turned-up nose, much more like a snout than a real nose. And its eyes were getting extremely small for a baby. Alice did not like the look of the thing at all.

"If you're going to turn into a pig," said Alice,

"I'll have nothing more to do with you." The poor little thing sobbed again (or grunted—it was impossible to say which), and they sat in silence for a while.

Alice was thinking to herself, "What am I to do with this creature when I get it home?" when it grunted again—so loudly that she looked down into its face in surprise. This time there could be *no* mistake about it. It was a pig, and she thought it was silly for her to carry it any more.

So she put the little creature down and felt relieved to see it run away into the woods. "If it had grown up," she said to herself, "it would have made an ugly child—but it makes rather a handsome pig, I think." Alice began to think about pigs and such and hardly noticed that she had wandered back into the woods.

She was a little surprised to see the Cheshire Cat sitting on a branch of a tree just a few yards away.

The Cat grinned when it saw Alice. It looked friendly, but it had long claws and many teeth, so Alice felt it needed to be treated with respect.

"Cheshire Puss," she began, rather carefully. She wasn't sure whether it would like the name. It grinned a little wider. "Would you tell me, please, which way to go from here?"

"That depends on *where* you want to go," said the Cat.

"I don't much care where—" said Alice.

"Then it doesn't matter which way you walk," said the Cat.

"—so long as I get *somewhere*," Alice added.

"Oh, you're sure to do that," said the Cat, "if you only walk long enough."

Alice knew that was true, so she tried another question. "What sort of people live around here?"

"In *that* direction," the Cat said, waving its right paw around, "lives a Hatter. In *that* direction," waving the other paw, "lives a March Hare. Visit either you like. They're both mad."

"But I don't want to go among mad people," Alice remarked.

"Oh, you can't help that," said the Cat. "We're all mad here. I'm mad. You're mad."

"How do you know I'm mad?" said Alice.

"You must be," said the Cat, "or you wouldn't have come here."

Alice didn't think that proved anything at all. "And how do you know that you're mad?"

"To begin with," said the Cat, "a dog's not mad. Do you agree?"

"I suppose so," said Alice.

"Well, then," the Cat went on, "you see, a dog growls when it's angry, and wags its tail when it's pleased. Now, *I* growl when I'm pleased, and wag my tail when I'm angry. Therefore I'm mad."

"I call it purring, not growling," said Alice.

"Call it what you like," said the Cat. "Do you play croquet with the Queen today?"

"I would like to very much," said Alice, "but I haven't been invited yet."

"You'll see me there," said the Cat, and then it vanished.

Alice was not surprised at this. She was getting used to strange things happening. While she was looking at the place where the Cat had been, it suddenly appeared again.

"By the way, what became of the baby?" said the Cat. "I'd nearly forgotten to ask."

"It turned into a pig," Alice quietly said.

"I thought it would," said the Cat, and it vanished again.

Alice waited a little, expecting to see it again, but it did not appear. After a minute or two she began walking in the direction in which the March Hare lived.

She looked up, and there was the Cat again, sitting on a branch of a tree.

"I wish you wouldn't keep appearing and vanishing so suddenly," said Alice.

"As you wish," said the Cat. This time it vanished quite slowly, beginning with the end of its tail, and ending with the grin. His grin remained some time after the rest of it had gone.

"Well! I've often seen a cat without a grin," thought Alice, "but a grin without a cat! It's the most curious thing I ever saw in my life!"

She had not gone far before she found the March Hare's house. The house had chimneys shaped like ears and a roof covered with fur. It was a large house, and she didn't want to go any closer until she had grown to about two feet high. So she nibbled on the left-hand bit of mushroom before she walked toward it. "What if the March Hare really *is* mad?" she said nervously. "I almost wish I'd gone to see the Hatter instead!"

CHAPTER SEVEN

A Mad Tea Party

There was a large table under a tree in front of the house, and the March Hare and the Hatter were having tea. A Dormouse was sitting between them, fast asleep. The other two were using it as a cushion and resting their elbows on it. "It must be very uncomfortable for the Dormouse," thought Alice, "but, being asleep, I suppose it doesn't care."

The table was long and was set for company, but the three were all crowded together at one corner of it. "There's no room! No room!" they cried out when they saw Alice coming.

"There's *plenty* of room!" said Alice, and she sat

down in a large armchair at one end of the table.

"Have some lemonade," the March Hare said invitingly.

Alice looked all round the table, but there was nothing on it but tea. "I don't see any lemonade," she remarked.

"There isn't any," said the March Hare.

"Then it wasn't very nice of you to offer it," said Alice.

"It wasn't very nice of you to sit down without being invited," said the March Hare.

"I didn't know it was *your* table," said Alice. "It has plenty of room."

"Your hair needs cutting," said the Hatter. He had been looking at Alice for some time with great interest, and this was his first comment.

"You should learn not to make personal remarks," Alice said. "It's very rude."

The Hatter opened his eyes very wide, but all he *said* was, "Why is a raven like a writing desk?"

"Good, now we will have some fun!" thought Alice. "I'm glad they've begun asking riddles." She said aloud, "I think I can guess that."

"Do you mean that you think you can find out the answer to it?" said the March Hare.

"Exactly so," said Alice.

"Then you should say what you mean," the March Hare went on.

"I do," Alice replied. "At least I mean what I say—that's the same thing, you know."

"It's not the same thing!" said the Hatter. "You might as well say that 'I see what I eat' is the same thing as 'I eat what I see'!"

"Or, you might as well say," added the March Hare, "that 'I like what I get' is the same thing as 'I get what I like'!"

"Or, you might as well say," added the Dormouse, who seemed to be talking in his sleep, "that 'I breathe when I sleep' is the same thing as 'I sleep when I breathe'!"

"It *is* the same thing with *you*," said the Hatter, and everyone was silent for a minute.

Alice thought over what she could remember about ravens and writing desks, which wasn't much.

The Hatter was the first to break the silence. "What day of the month is it?" he said to Alice. He had taken his watch out of his pocket and was looking at it. Then he shook it and held it to his ear.

Alice thought to herself a little and then said, "The fourth."

"Two days wrong!" sighed the Hatter.

Alice looked over his shoulder with interest. "What a funny watch!" she remarked. "It tells the day of the month, and doesn't tell what o'clock it is!"

"Why should it?" muttered the Hatter. "Does *your* watch tell you what *year* it is?"

"Of course not," Alice replied, "but that's because it stays the same year for such a long time."

"Which is just the same case as *mine*," said the Hatter.

"I don't quite understand you," Alice said, as politely as she could.

"The Dormouse is asleep again," said the Hatter, and he poured a little hot tea upon its nose.

The Dormouse shook its head and said, without opening its eyes, "Of course, of course— just what I was going to say myself."

"Have you guessed the riddle yet?" the Hatter said, turning to Alice again.

"No. I give up," Alice replied. "What's the answer?"

"I haven't the slightest idea," said the Hatter.

"Nor I," said the March Hare.

Alice sighed. "I think you should do something better with the time," she said, "than waste it asking riddles that have no answers."

"If you knew Time as well as I do," said the Hatter, "you wouldn't talk about wasting *it*. Time is a *him*."

"I don't know what you mean," said Alice.

"Of course you don't!" the Hatter said, tossing his head. "I bet you never even spoke to Time!"

"No, I haven't," Alice replied, "but I know I have to beat time when I learn music."

"Ah! That's it!" said the Hatter. "Time won't stand beating. Now, if you only kept on good terms with him, he'd do almost anything you liked with the clock. But, alas." The Hatter shook his head mournfully. "I had an argument with Time last March—just before *he* went mad, you know—" (pointing with his teaspoon at the March Hare). "It was at the great concert given by the Queen of Hearts, and I had to sing:

> *Twinkle, twinkle, little bat!*
> *How I wonder what you're at!*

Do you know the song?"

"I've heard something like it," said Alice.

"It goes on, you know," the Hatter continued, "in this way:

> *Up above the world you fly,*
> *Like a tea tray in the sky.*
> *Twinkle, twinkle—*"

Here the Dormouse shook itself, and began singing in its sleep, "*Twinkle, twinkle, twinkle,*

twinkle—" and went on so long that they had to pinch it to make it stop.

"Well, I'd hardly finished the first verse," said the Hatter, "when the Queen jumped up and yelled out, 'He's murdering the Time! Off with his head!' "

"How terrible!" exclaimed Alice.

"And ever since that," the Hatter went on in a mournful tone, "he won't do a thing I ask! It's always six o'clock now."

"Is that the reason so many tea things are put out here?" she asked.

"Yes, that's it," said the Hatter with a sigh. "It's always tea time, and we've no time to wash the things in between."

"Then you keep moving around the table, I suppose?" said Alice.

"Exactly," said the Hatter. "As the things get used."

"But what happens when you come to the beginning again?" Alice asked.

"Let's change the subject," the March Hare interrupted, yawning. "I'm getting tired of this. I vote the young lady tells us a story."

"I'm afraid I don't know one," said Alice.

"Then the Dormouse shall!" they both cried. "Wake up, Dormouse!" And they pinched it on both sides at once.

The Dormouse slowly opened his eyes. "I wasn't asleep," he said in a hoarse, feeble voice. "I heard every word you fellows were saying."

"Tell us a story!" said the March Hare.

"Yes, please do!" pleaded Alice.

"And be quick about it," added the Hatter, "or you'll be asleep again before it's done."

"Once upon a time there were three little sisters," the Dormouse began in a great hurry, "and their names were Elsie, Lacie, and Tillie, and they lived at the bottom of a well—"

"What did they live on?" asked Alice.

"They lived on treacle," said the Dormouse, after thinking a minute or two.

"They couldn't have done that, you know," Alice gently remarked. "Treacle is just syrup. They'd have been ill."

"So they were," said the Dormouse. "*Very* ill."

"But why did they live at the bottom of a well?" Alice asked.

"Have some more tea," the March Hare said to Alice, very sincerely.

"I haven't had *any* yet," Alice replied, "so I can't have any more."

"You mean you can't have any *less*," said the Hatter. "It's very easy to take *more* than nothing."

Alice did not know what to say, so she poured some tea and took some bread-and-butter and then turned to the Dormouse and asked again, "Why did they live at the bottom of a well?"

"I want a clean cup," interrupted the Hatter. "Everyone move over one place."

He moved on as he spoke, and the Dormouse followed him. The March Hare moved into the Dormouse's place, and Alice unwillingly took the place of the March Hare. The Hatter was the only one who got a clean cup from the move. Alice was worse off than before, as the March Hare had just spilled milk into his plate.

The Dormouse had closed its eyes by this time and was going off to sleep. The Hatter pinched it and it woke up with a little shriek, and went on: "They were in the well learning to draw. They drew things that begin with M, such as mouse-traps, and the moon, and memory, and muchness— you know, you say things are 'much of a muchness,' but did you ever see a drawing of a muchness?"

"I am very confused," said Alice, "I don't think—"

"Then you shouldn't talk," said the Hatter.

Alice had *certainly* had enough. She got up and walked off. The Dormouse fell asleep instantly, and neither of the others cared or noticed that Alice had gone. She looked back once or twice, hoping they would call her back. The last time she looked she saw them trying to put the Dormouse into the teapot.

"I'll never go *there* again!" said Alice, as she made her way through the woods. Then she noticed that one of the trees had a door leading right into it. "That's very curious," she thought. "I may as well go in it." And in she went.

Once more she found herself back in the long hallway and close to the little glass table. "This time I'll get this right," she said, and took the little golden key off the table and unlocked the door that led into the garden. Then she nibbled on the right-hand bit of mushroom, until she was about a foot high. She walked through the little door, and *at last* found herself in the beautiful garden.

CHAPTER EIGHT

The Queen's Croquet Ground

A large rose tree stood near the entrance of the garden. The roses growing on it were white, but there were three gardeners busily painting the roses red.

"Why, they look just like playing cards," thought Alice. This was very strange, and she went closer to watch them.

"Look out now, Five! Don't splash paint on me like that!"

"I couldn't help it," said Five. "Seven bumped my elbow."

Seven looked up and said, "That's right, Five! Always blame it on others!"

"*You'd* better not talk!" said Five. "I heard the Queen say yesterday you deserved to be beheaded!"

"What for?" said the one who had spoken first.

"That's none of *your* business, Two!" said Seven.

"Yes, it *is* his business!" said Five. "And I'll tell him—it was for bringing the cook tulip-roots instead of onions."

Seven flung down his brush, and had just begun, "Well, of all the unfair things—" when his eye suddenly fell upon Alice, as she stood watching them. He stopped himself quickly. The others saw her, too, and all of them bowed.

"Would you tell me, please," said Alice, "why you are painting those roses?"

Two began in a low voice, "Well, you see, miss, this should have been a *red* rose tree, and we put a white one in by mistake. If the Queen found out, we would have our heads cut off. So we're doing our best to—" At that moment Five, who had been looking around the garden, called out, "The Queen! The Queen!" The three gardeners instantly threw themselves flat upon their faces. There was a sound of many footsteps, and Alice looked around to see the Queen.

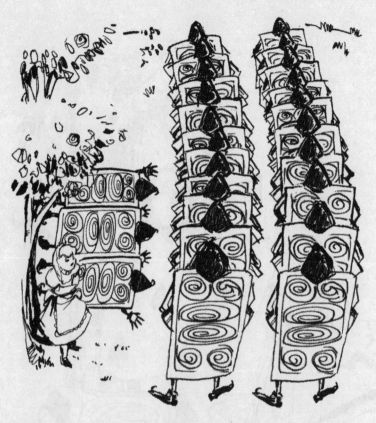

First came ten soldiers carrying clubs, who also looked like cards, with their hands and feet at the corners. Next came ten courtiers, decorated all over with diamonds. They walked two by two, as the soldiers did. After these came the royal children, with hearts upon their garments. There were ten of them, and they were jumping along hand in hand. Next came the guests, mostly Kings and Queens, and among them Alice recognized the White Rabbit. It was smiling at everything that was said, and went by without noticing her. Then followed the Knave of Hearts, carrying the King's crown on a red velvet cushion. And, last of all, at the end of the grand procession, came THE KING AND QUEEN OF HEARTS.

Alice wasn't sure if she should lie down on her face like the gardeners. She could not remember a rule about lying down for a procession.

"And besides," she thought, "what is the use of a procession if people have to lie down upon their faces? Then they are not able to see it." So she stood still where she was, and waited.

When the procession came to Alice, they all stopped and looked at her. The Queen said, "Who is this?" to the Knave of Hearts, who only bowed and smiled in reply.

"Fool!" said the Queen, tossing her head, and turning to Alice. "What is your name, child?"

"My name is Alice, your Majesty," said Alice very politely, as she thought, "Why, they're only a pack of cards. I don't need to be afraid of them!"

"And who are *these*?" said the Queen, pointing to the three gardeners who were lying face down in front of the rose tree.

"How should *I* know?" said Alice, surprised at her own courage. "It's no business of *mine*."

The Queen turned red with fury and screamed, "Off with her head! Off—"

"Nonsense!" said Alice, very loudly, and the Queen was silent.

The King laid his hand upon the Queen's arm, and quietly said, "My dear, she is only a child!"

The Queen turned angrily away from him, and said to the Knave, "Turn them over!"

The Knave carefully turned them over with one foot.

"Get up!" said the Queen in a loud voice, and the three gardeners instantly jumped up. They began bowing to the King, the Queen, the royal children, and everybody else.

"Stop that!" screamed the Queen. "You're making me dizzy." She turned to the rose tree and said, "What *have* you been doing here?"

"Your Majesty," said Two, going down on one knee as he spoke, "we were trying—"

"*I* see!" said the Queen, who was looking at

the roses. "Off with their heads!"

The royal group left. Three of the soldiers stayed behind to execute the gardeners, who ran to Alice for protection.

"You won't be executed!" said Alice, and she put them into a large flowerpot that stood near. The three soldiers wandered about looking for them, and then quietly marched off after the others.

"Are their heads off?" shouted the Queen.

"Their heads are gone, your Majesty!" the soldiers shouted in reply.

"Can you play croquet?"

The soldiers were silent, and looked at Alice, as the question was meant for her.

"Yes!" shouted Alice.

"Come on, then!" yelled the Queen, and Alice joined the procession.

"It's a nice day!" said a voice at her side. It was the White Rabbit, peeping into her face.

"Very," said Alice. "Where's the Duchess?"

"Shhh!" said the Rabbit. He looked over his shoulder and then raised himself up on tiptoe so he could whisper in her ear. "She's been arrested and will be executed."

"What for?" said Alice.

"Did you say 'What a pity!'?" the Rabbit asked.

"No, I didn't," said Alice. "I said, 'What for?' "

"She boxed the Queen's ears—" the Rabbit began. Alice laughed. "Shhh!" the Rabbit whispered. "The Queen will hear you! You see, the Duchess was late, and the Queen said—"

"Get in your places!" shouted the Queen. People ran around in all directions. They finally settled down and the game began.

Alice had never seen such a strange croquet ground. There were lots of hills and holes. The balls were live hedgehogs and the mallets were live flamingos. The soldiers stood on their hands and feet to make the arches.

Alice tried to hold her flamingo still, but it kept twisting around so it could look at Alice. She couldn't help laughing. When she finally got the flamingo to hold still, she looked down and found that the hedgehog had run away. It was a hard and confusing game. The players played at the same time. No one took turns. They argued about everything, and the Queen went stomping around screaming, "Off with his head!" or "Off with her head!" every minute.

Alice began to feel very uneasy. She had not

yet had an argument with the Queen, but she knew that it might happen any minute.

She started looking around for a way to leave, when she noticed a curious appearance in the air—a grin! "It's the Cheshire Cat," she said to herself. "Now I will have somebody to talk to."

"How are you doing?" said the Cat, as soon as there was enough mouth for it to speak with.

Alice waited till the eyes appeared, and then nodded. "There's no use speaking to it till its ears have come," she thought. In another minute the whole head appeared, and then Alice put down her flamingo. She began to tell the Cat about the game. The Cat seemed to think his head was enough, and no more of it appeared.

"I don't think they play fairly," Alice said, "and they all argue, and they don't have any rules. You have no idea how confusing it is using flamingos, and hedgehogs, and arches that walk away."

"How do you like the Queen?" asked the Cat.

"Not at all," said Alice. "She's so—" Just then she noticed that the Queen was close behind her, listening. She went on, "—likely to win, that it's not worth finishing the game."

The Queen smiled and walked by.

ALICE'S ADVENTURES
IN WONDERLAND

"Whom *are* you talking to?" said the King, walking up to Alice, and looking at the Cat's head with curiosity.

"It's a friend of mine, a Cheshire Cat," said Alice.

"I don't like the looks of it," said the King, "but, it may kiss my hand if it likes."

"I'd rather not," the Cat remarked.

"Don't be disrespectful," said the King, "and don't look at me like that!" He got behind Alice as he spoke.

"A cat can look at a king," said Alice. "I read that in a book somewhere."

"Well, it must be removed," said the King and he called the Queen. "My dear! I wish you would have this cat removed!"

The Queen had one way of settling problems, great or small. "Off with his head!" she said, without even looking up.

"I'll get the executioner myself," said the King, and he hurried off. He quickly returned with the executioner and a crowd began to gather around.

A disagreement began between the King, the executioner, and the Queen. They were all talking at once, while the entire crowd was silent and uncomfortable.

Alice asked if she could help settle the question. They all started speaking to her at once, so she found it very hard to know exactly what they said.

The executioner's argument was that you couldn't cut off a head unless there was a body to cut it off from. The King's argument was that anything that had a head could be beheaded. The Queen's argument was that if something weren't done soon then she'd have *everybody* executed.

Alice could not think of anything else to say but "The Cat belongs to the Duchess, you'd better ask her about it."

"She's in prison," the Queen said to the executioner. "Bring her here." And the executioner went off like an arrow.

The Cat's head began fading away the moment the executioner was gone. By the time the executioner had come back with the Duchess, the Cat had disappeared completely. So the King and the executioner ran wildly up and down looking for the Cheshire Cat's head, while the rest of the party went back to the game.

CHAPTER NINE

The Mock Turtle's Story

"I am so glad to see you again!" said the Duchess, as she tucked her arm into Alice's, and they walked off together.

Alice was very glad to see she was in a good mood, and thought to herself that it was the pepper that had made her so mean when they met in the kitchen.

"You're thinking about something," said the Duchess, "and that makes you forget to talk. I can't tell you just now what the moral of that is, but I will remember it in a bit."

"Maybe it doesn't have a moral," Alice said.

"Tut, tut, child!" said the Duchess. "Everything

has a moral." And she squeezed closer to Alice's side.

Alice did not like being so close to her. The Duchess was very ugly, and she rested her chin right on Alice's shoulder—and it was a *very* pointy chin. Alice did not want to be rude, so she put up with the pain as best as she could.

"The game is going much better now," Alice managed to say.

"Yes, it is," said the Duchess, "and the moral of *that* is—'Oh, 'tis love, 'tis love that makes the world go round!' "

"Somebody said," Alice whispered, "that it's done by everybody minding their own business!"

"Ah, well! It means much the same thing," said the Duchess, "and the moral of *that* is—'Take care of the sense, and the sounds will take care of themselves.' "

"How fond she is of finding morals in things!" Alice thought to herself.

"I'm sure you're wondering why I don't put my arm around your waist," the Duchess said after a pause. "The reason is that I'm worried about the temper of your flamingo. Should I try?"

"He might bite," Alice cautiously replied.

"Very true," said the Duchess. "Flamingos and mustard both bite. And the moral of *that* is—'Birds of a feather flock together.'"

"Only, mustard isn't a bird," Alice remarked.

"Right, as usual," said the Duchess. "What a clear way you have of putting things!"

"It's a mineral, I *think*," said Alice.

"Of course it is," said the Duchess. "There's a large mustard mine near here. And the moral of *that* is—'The more there is of mine, the less there is of yours.' "

"Oh, I know!" exclaimed Alice, who didn't really hear her last remark. "Mustard is a vegetable."

"Thinking again?" the Duchess asked, with another dig of her pointy little chin.

"I have a right to think," said Alice sharply, for she was beginning to feel a little uncomfortable.

"Of course," said the Duchess. "Just about as much right as pigs have to fly. And the mor—"

The Duchess's voice died away and her arm that was linked with Alice's began to tremble. Alice looked up, and there stood the Queen in front of them, with her arms folded, frowning.

"A fine day, your Majesty!" the Duchess began in a low, weak voice.

"I'm warning you," shouted the Queen, "either you or your head must be off! It's your choice!"

The Duchess made her choice, and was gone in no time.

"Let's go on with the game," the Queen said to Alice. Alice was much too frightened to say a word. She slowly followed the Queen back to the croquet ground.

The other guests were resting in the shade, but the moment they saw the Queen, they hurried back to the game.

The whole time they were playing, the Queen never stopped arguing with the other players and shouting, "Off with his head!" or "Off with her head!" After a while, the soldiers (who had to stop being arches) had taken away all the players to be executed except for the King, the Queen, and Alice.

Then the Queen said to Alice, "Have you seen the Mock Turtle yet?"

"No," said Alice. "I don't even know what a Mock Turtle is."

"It's the thing Mock Turtle Soup is made from," said the Queen.

"I never saw one, or heard of one," said Alice.

"Come on, then," said the Queen, "and he shall tell you his history."

As they walked off together, Alice heard the King say in a low voice to everyone, "You are all pardoned."

They came to a Gryphon, lying fast asleep in the sun. (If you don't know what a Gryphon is, look at the picture.) "Get up, you lazy thing!" said the Queen, "and take this young lady to meet the Mock Turtle. I must go back and finish my game," and she walked off, leaving Alice alone with the Gryphon. Alice did not like the looks of the creature, but she thought it would be much safer to stay with it than to go with the Queen.

The Gryphon sat up and rubbed its eyes. Then it watched the Queen until she was out of sight. It chuckled. "What fun!" said the Gryphon.

"What is the fun?" Alice asked.

"Why, *she*," said the Gryphon. "It's all make-believe. She never executes nobody, you know. Come on!"

They did not go far before they saw the Mock Turtle sitting sad and lonely on a little ledge of rock. Alice could hear him sighing as if his heart were breaking.

"Why is he so sad?" she asked the Gryphon. The Gryphon answered in almost the same words he had used before. "It's all make-believe. He hasn't got no sorrow, you know. Come on!"

So they went up to the Mock Turtle, who looked at them with large eyes full of tears but said nothing.

"This here young lady," said the Gryphon, "she wants for to know you, she do."

"I'll tell her all about myself," said the Mock Turtle in a deep, hollow tone. "Sit down, both of you, and don't speak a word till I've finished."

So they sat down, and nobody spoke for some minutes.

"Once," said the Mock Turtle, with a deep sigh, "I was a real Turtle."

Then there was a very long silence. Alice was ready to get up and leave and tell the Mock Turtle, "Thank you, sir, for your interesting story," but she could not help thinking there *must* be more to come, so she waited and said nothing.

"When we were little," the Mock Turtle went on at last, still sobbing a little now and then, "we went to school in the sea. The master was an old Turtle—we used to call him Tortoise because he *taught us*. Yes, we went to school in the sea, though you may not believe it—"

"I never said I didn't!" interrupted Alice.

"You did," said the Mock Turtle.

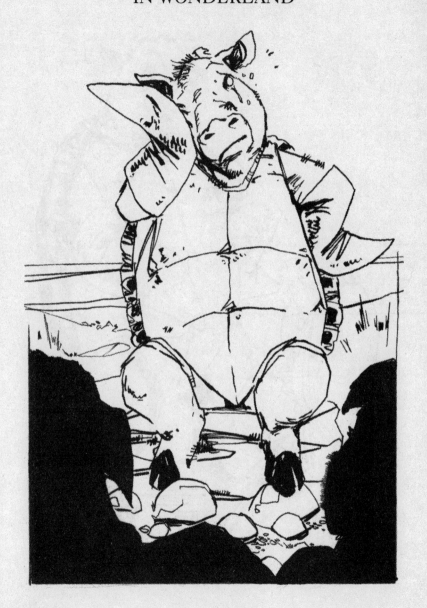

"Hold your tongue!" added the Gryphon, before Alice could speak again. The Mock Turtle went on.

"We had the best education. In fact, we went to school every day—"

"*I've* been to school, too," said Alice. "You needn't be so proud of that."

"With extras?" asked the Mock Turtle.

"Yes," said Alice. "We learned French and music."

"And Washing?" said the Mock Turtle.

"Certainly not!" said Alice.

"Ah! Then *yours* wasn't a really good school," said the Mock Turtle in a tone of great relief.

"How many hours a day did you do lessons?" said Alice, in a hurry to change the subject.

"Ten hours the first day," said the Mock Turtle, "nine the next, and so on."

"What a curious plan!" exclaimed Alice.

"That's the reason they're called lessons," the Gryphon remarked, "because they *lessen* from day to day."

This was a new idea to Alice. She thought about it before she said, "Then the eleventh day must have been a holiday?"

"Of course it was," said the Mock Turtle.

"And what did you do on the twelfth?" Alice went on eagerly.

"That's enough about lessons," the Gryphon interrupted in a very decided tone. "Tell her something about the games now."

CHAPTER TEN

The Lobster Quadrille

The Mock Turtle sighed deeply, and drew the back of one flapper across his eyes. He looked at Alice and tried to speak, but for a minute or two sobs choked his voice. "Same as if he had a bone in his throat," said the Gryphon, and he started shaking him and punching him in the back. At last the Mock Turtle got back his voice, and, with tears running down his cheeks, he went on.

"You may not have lived much under the sea." ("I haven't," said Alice.) "Then you were never even introduced to a lobster." ("No, never.") "So you can have no idea what a delightful thing a Lobster Quadrille is!"

"No, indeed," said Alice. "What sort of a square dance is it?"

"Well," said the Gryphon, "you first form a line along the seashore—"

"Two lines!" cried the Mock Turtle. "Seals, turtles, salmon, and so on. Then, when you've cleared all the jellyfish out of the way—"

"*That* generally takes some time," interrupted the Gryphon.

"—you step forward twice—"

"Each with a lobster as a partner!" cried the Gryphon.

"Of course," the Mock Turtle said. "Step forward twice, with your partners—"

"—change lobsters, and go backward the same way," continued the Gryphon.

"Then, you know," the Mock Turtle went on, "you throw the—"

"The lobsters!" shouted the Gryphon, jumping into the air.

"—as far out to sea as you can—"

"Swim after them!" screamed the Gryphon.

"Turn a somersault in the sea!" cried the Mock Turtle, jumping wildly about.

"Change lobsters again!" yelled the Gryphon at the top of its voice.

"Swim back to land again, and—that's all," said the Mock Turtle, suddenly dropping its voice. The two creatures, who had been jumping around like mad, sat down again very sadly and quietly, and looked at Alice.

"It must be a very pretty dance," said Alice timidly.

"Would you like to see a little of it?" said the Mock Turtle.

"Yes, I would," said Alice.

"Come on, let's try the first part!" said the Mock Turtle to the Gryphon. "We can do without lobsters, you know. Which shall sing?"

"Oh, *you* sing," said the Gryphon. "I've forgotten the words."

So they began solemnly dancing round and round Alice, every now and then stepping on her toes. They waved their forepaws to mark the time, while the Mock Turtle sang very slowly and sadly.

"Will you walk a little faster?"
said a whiting to a snail.
"There's a porpoise close behind us,
and he's treading on my tail.
See how eagerly the lobsters
and the turtles all advance!
They are waiting on the shingle—
will you come and join the dance?
Will you, won't you, will you,
won't you, will you join the dance?
Will you, won't you, will you,
won't you, won't you join the dance?"

They sang and danced and danced and sang and all at once it was over.

ALICE'S ADVENTURES IN WONDERLAND

"Thank you, it's a very interesting dance to watch," said Alice, feeling very glad that it was over at last. "And I do so like that curious song."

"Curious indeed," said the Gryphon, "but it all makes perfect sense, when one says the words aloud. And now, tell us some of *your* adventures."

"I could tell you my adventures—beginning from this morning," said Alice a little timidly, "but it's no use going back to yesterday, because I was a different person then."

"Explain all that," said the Mock Turtle.

"No, no! The adventures first," said the Gryphon impatiently. "Explanations take too much time."

So Alice began telling them about her adventures beginning with when she first saw the White Rabbit. The two creatures sat very close to her, one on each side, and opened their eyes and mouths *very* wide. It made her quite nervous, but she felt better as she went on with her story. The Mock Turtle and the Gryphon kept quiet until she finished. After she was done, the Mock Turtle drew in a long breath and said, "That's a very curious story."

"It's about as curious as it can be," said the Gryphon. "Shall we try another part of the Lobster Quadrille? Or would you like the Mock Turtle to sing you a song?"

"Oh, I would love to hear a song," Alice replied, so eagerly that the Gryphon said, in a rather offended tone, "Hm! Well, that is *your* choice! Sing her '*Turtle Soup*,' will you, old fellow?"

The Mock Turtle sighed deeply, and began, in a voice sometimes choked with sobs, to sing this:

Beautiful Soup, so rich and green,
Waiting in a hot tureen!
Who for such dainties would not stoop?
Soup of the evening, beautiful Soup!
Soup of the evening, beautiful Soup!
Beau—ootiful Soo—oop!
Beau—ootiful Soo—oop!
Soo—oop of the e—e—evening,
Beautiful, beautiful Soup!

Beautiful Soup! Who cares for fish,
Game, or any other dish?
Who would not give all else for two-p
-Ennies worth only of beautiful Soup?
Pennies worth only of beautiful Soup?
Beau—ootiful Soo—oop!
Beau—ootiful Soo—oop!
Soo—oop of the e—e—evening,
Beautiful, beauti—FUL SOUP!

"Sing the chorus again!" cried the Gryphon, and the Mock Turtle had just begun to repeat it, when a cry of "The trial's beginning!" was heard off in the distance.

"Come on!" cried the Gryphon. Taking Alice by the hand, it hurried off without waiting for the end of the song.

"What trial is it?" Alice panted as she ran, but the Gryphon only answered, "Come on!" and ran all the faster. Behind them they could hear the Mock Turtle still singing:

Soo—oop of the e—e—evening,
Beautiful, beautiful Soup!

CHAPTER ELEVEN

Who Stole the Tarts?

The King and Queen of Hearts were seated on their thrones when the Gryphon and Alice arrived. There was a large crowd around them—all sorts of little birds and beasts, as well as the whole pack of cards. The Knave was standing before them, in chains and with a soldier on each side to guard him. Next to the King was the White Rabbit. He had a trumpet in one hand and a scroll in the other.

In the middle of the court was a table, with a large dish of tarts upon it. They looked so good that it made Alice hungry when she looked at them. "I wish they'd get the trial done," she thought, "and hand out the refreshments!"

But there didn't seem to be a chance this would happen, so she started looking around to pass the time.

Alice had never been in a court of justice before, but she had read all about them in books and seemed to know the names of nearly everything there.

"That's the judge," she thought, looking at the King. He did not look comfortable at all. "And that's the jury box, and those twelve creatures—" (some of them were animals, and some were birds) "—are the jurors."

The twelve jurors were all writing with pencils on little slates.

"What are they doing?" Alice whispered to the Gryphon. "There can't be anything to write down yet. The trial has not begun!"

"They're putting down their names," the Gryphon whispered in reply, "so they won't forget them before the end of the trial."

"Silly things!" Alice began in a loud voice, but she stopped when the White Rabbit cried out, "Silence in the court!"

The King put on his glasses and looked around to see who was talking.

Alice saw that all the jurors were writing down "Silly things!" on their slates. She also saw that one of them didn't know how to spell "silly." He had to ask his neighbor for help. "Those slates will be filled with nonsense before the trial is over!" thought Alice.

"Herald, read the charges!" said the King.

The White Rabbit blew three blasts on the trumpet, and then unrolled the scroll, and read:

> *"The Queen of Hearts, she made some tarts,*
> *All on a summer day.*
> *The Knave of Hearts, he stole those tarts,*
> *And took them quite away!"*

"Consider your verdict," the King said to the jury.

"Not yet, not yet!" the Rabbit interrupted. "There's a great deal to come before that!"

"Call the first witness," said the King. The White Rabbit blew three blasts on the trumpet, and called out, "First witness!"

The first witness was the Hatter. He came in with a teacup in one hand and a piece of bread-and-butter in the other.

"I beg pardon, your Majesty," the Hatter began, "for bringing these in, but I hadn't finished my tea when I was sent for."

"You ought to have finished," said the King. "When did you begin?"

The Hatter looked at the March Hare, who had followed him into the court, arm-in-arm with the Dormouse. "Fourteenth of March, I think it was," he said.

"Fifteenth," said the March Hare.

"Sixteenth," added the Dormouse.

"Write that down," the King said to the jury. They wrote down all three dates on their slates, and then added them up.

"Take off your hat," the King told the Hatter.

"It isn't mine," said the Hatter.

"*Stolen!*" the King exclaimed. The jury made a note.

"I keep them to sell," the Hatter added. "I have none of my own. I'm a hatter."

Here the Queen stared very hard at the Hatter. He turned pale.

"Give your evidence," said the King, "and don't be nervous, or I'll have you executed on the spot."

This did not make the witness feel

comfortable at all. He kept shifting from one foot to the other, looking uneasily at the Queen. He was so nervous he bit a large piece out of his teacup instead of the bread-and-butter.

At this moment Alice felt very strange. She was beginning to grow *larger* again. She thought at first that she should get up and leave the court, but she decided to stay as long as there was room for her.

"I wish you wouldn't squeeze so close to me," said the Dormouse, who was sitting next to her. "I can hardly breathe."

"I can't help it," said Alice. "I'm growing."

"You have no right to grow *here*," said the Dormouse.

"Don't talk nonsense," said Alice. "You know, you're growing too."

"Yes, but I grow at a reasonable pace," said the Dormouse.

All this time the Queen had been staring hard at the Hatter. "Isn't this the singer from the last concert who murdered the Time?" she asked an officer. The Hatter trembled so much that he shook both his shoes off.

"Give your evidence," the King repeated

angrily, "or I'll have you executed, whether you're nervous or not."

"I'm a poor man, your Majesty," the Hatter began, in a trembling voice, "and I had just begun my tea—about a week or so ago—and what with the bread-and-butter getting so thin—and the twinkling of the tea—"

"The twinkling of the *what*?" said the King.

"It began with the *tea*," the Hatter replied.

"Of course twinkling *begins* with a T!" said the King sharply. "Do you take me for a dunce? Go on!"

"I'm a poor man—" said the Hatter.

Then the miserable Hatter dropped his teacup and bread-and-butter and went down on one knee. "I'm a poor man, your Majesty," he began again.

"You're a *very* poor *speaker*," said the King.

One of the guinea pigs cheered, and was immediately suppressed by the officers of the court. (Suppressed is a hard word, so I will just explain to you what they did. They had a large bag, which tied at the top with strings. They slipped the guinea pig *head first* into the bag—and then sat on it.)

"I'm glad I've seen that done," thought Alice. "I never understood what it meant until now."

"If that's all you know about it, you may stand down," continued the King.

"I can't go no lower," said the Hatter. "I'm on the floor, as it is."

"Then you may *sit* down," the King replied.

Here the other guinea pig cheered, and was suppressed.

"There, that finishes the guinea pigs!" thought Alice. "Now we will get more done."

"I'd rather finish my tea," said the Hatter, looking nervously at the Queen.

"You may go," said the King, and the Hatter quickly left the court, without even putting on his shoes.

"—and just take his head off outside," the Queen said to one of the officers, but the Hatter was out of sight before the officer could get to the door.

"Call the next witness!" said the King.

The next witness was the Duchess's cook. She carried the pepper box in her hand. Alice guessed who it was, even before she got into the court, by the way people near the door began sneezing all at once.

"Give your evidence," said the King.

"Shan't," said the cook.

The King looked nervously at the White Rabbit, who said in a low voice, "Your Majesty *must* question this witness."

"Well, if I must, I must," the King said, folding his arms and frowning at the cook until his eyes were completely crossed. He said in a deep voice, "What are tarts made of?"

"Pepper," said the cook.

"Treacle," said a sleepy voice behind her.

"Collar that Dormouse," the Queen shrieked out. "Behead that Dormouse! Turn that Dormouse out of court! Suppress him! Pinch him! Off with his whiskers!"

For a few minutes the whole court was in confusion. They chased the Dormouse out, and, by the time they had settled down again, the cook had disappeared.

"Oh, never mind!" said the King, with great relief. "Call the next witness." He turned to the Queen and said, "Really, my dear, *you* must question the next witness. It makes my forehead ache!"

Alice watched the White Rabbit as he fumbled over the list. She was very curious to see what the next witness would be like. "They haven't got much evidence *yet*," she said to herself. Imagine her surprise, when the White Rabbit read out, at the top of his shrill little voice, the name:

"Alice!"

CHAPTER TWELVE

Alice's Evidence

"Here!" cried Alice, forgetting how large she had grown in the last few minutes. She jumped up in such a hurry that she tipped over the jury box with the edge of her skirt, sending all the jurymen onto the heads of the crowd below. There they lay sprawling around.

"Oh, I *beg* your pardon!" she exclaimed, and began picking them up again as fast as she could.

"The trial cannot proceed," said the King in a very stern voice, "until all the jurymen are back in their proper places—*all*," he repeated, looking hard at Alice.

Alice looked at the jury box and saw that she

had put the Lizard in head downward. The poor little thing was waving its tail all around—unable to move. Alice lifted it and put it right. After the jury had a moment to recover, they quickly started writing out a history of the accident. The Lizard, too overcome to do anything, sat with its mouth open, gazing up into the roof of the court.

"What do you know about this business?" the King said to Alice.

"Nothing," said Alice.

"Nothing *whatever*?" persisted the King.

"Nothing whatever," said Alice.

"That's very important," the King said, turning to the jury. They were just beginning to write this down on their slates, when the White Rabbit interrupted. "*Un*important, your Majesty means, of course," he said in a very respectful tone, but frowning and making faces at him as he spoke.

"*Un*important, of course, I meant," the King said, and then went on mumbling to himself, "important—unimportant—unimportant—important—" as if he were trying to decide which word sounded best.

Some of the jury wrote it down "important,"

and some "unimportant." Alice could see this, "but it doesn't matter a bit," she thought to herself.

At this moment the King, who had been for some time busily writing in his notebook, called out, "Silence!" and read out from his book, "Rule Number Forty-two. *All persons more than a mile high must leave the court.*"

Everybody looked at Alice.

"*I'm* not a mile high," said Alice.

"You are," said the King.

"Nearly two miles high," added the Queen.

"Well, I won't go," said Alice. "Besides, that's not a regular rule. You invented it just now."

"It's the oldest rule in the book," said the King.

"Then it should be Rule Number One, not Number Forty-two," said Alice.

The King turned pale, and shut his notebook. "Consider your verdict," he said to the jury, in a low, trembling voice.

"There's more evidence to come yet, please your Majesty," said the White Rabbit, jumping up in a great hurry. "This paper has just been picked up."

"What's in it?" said the Queen.

"I haven't opened it yet," said the White

Rabbit, "but it seems to be a letter, written by the prisoner to—to somebody."

"Whom is it to?" said one of the jurymen.

"To no one at all," said the White Rabbit. "In fact, there's nothing written on the *outside*." He unfolded the paper as he spoke, and added, "It isn't a letter, after all. It's a set of verses."

"Are they in the prisoner's handwriting?" asked another juryman.

"No, they're not," said the White Rabbit, "and that's the strangest thing about it."

"He must have copied somebody else's handwriting," said the King.

"Please your Majesty," said the Knave, "I didn't write it, and they can't prove I did. There's no name signed at the end."

"If you didn't sign it," said the King, "that only makes the matter worse. You must have meant some mischief, or else you'd have signed your name like an honest man."

Everyone in the court started clapping. It was the first clever thing the King had said that day.

"That proves he's guilty," said the Queen.

"It proves nothing!" said Alice. "You don't even know what the verses are about!"

"Read them," said the King.

The White Rabbit put on his glasses. "Where shall I begin, please your Majesty?" he asked.

"Begin at the beginning," the King said solemnly, "and go on till you come to the end. Then stop."

There was silence while the White Rabbit read:

They told me you had been to her,
And mentioned me to him.
She gave me a good character,
But said I could not swim.

He sent them word I had not gone
(We know it to be true).
If she should push the matter on,
What would become of you?

I gave her one, they gave him two,
You gave us three or more.
They all returned from him to you,
Though they were mine before.

If I or she should chance to be
Involved in this affair,
He trusts to you to set them free,
Exactly as we were.

My notion was that you had been
(Before she had this fit)
An obstacle that came between
Him, and ourselves, and it.

Don't let him know she liked them best,
For this must ever be
A secret, kept from all the rest,
Between yourself and me.

"That's the most important piece of evidence we've heard yet," said the King, rubbing his hands together, "so now let the jury—"

"Is there *anyone* who can explain those verses?" asked Alice. (She had grown so large in the last few minutes that she wasn't afraid of interrupting him.) "I don't believe there's *any* meaning in it."

The jury all wrote down on their slates, "*She* doesn't believe there's *any* meaning in it."

"If there's no meaning in it," said the King, "that saves a lot of trouble, as we should not try to find any meaning. I don't know," he went on, spreading out the verses on his knee, and looking at them with one eye. "I seem to see some meaning in them, after all. —'*said I could not swim.*' You can't swim, can you?" he added, turning to the Knave.

The Knave shook his head sadly. "Do I look like it?" he said. (Which he certainly did *not*, being made entirely of cardboard.)

"All right, so far," said the King, and he looked over the verses, talking to himself. " '*We know it to be true*'—that's the jury, of course—'*If she should push the matter on*'—that must be the

Queen—'*What would become of you?*'—What, indeed!—'*I gave her one, they gave him two*'—why, that must be what he did with the tarts, you know—"

"But it goes on '*They all returned from him to you,*'" said Alice.

"And *there* they *are*!" said the King, pointing to the tarts on the table. "Nothing can be clearer than that. Then again—'*before she had this fit*'—you never had *fits*, my dear, I think?" he said to the Queen.

"Never!" said the Queen furiously, throwing an inkstand at the Lizard as she spoke.

"Then the words don't *fit* you," said the King, looking round the court with a smile. There was a dead silence.

"It's a pun!" the King added, and everybody laughed. "Let the jury give their verdict," the King said, for about the twentieth time that day.

"No, no!" said the Queen. "Punishment first—verdict afterward."

"Nonsense!" said Alice loudly. "The idea of having the punishment first!"

"Hold your tongue!" said the Queen, turning purple.

"I won't!" said Alice.

"Off with her head!" the Queen shouted at the top of her voice. Nobody moved.

"Who cares for *you*?" said Alice. (She had grown to her full size by this time.) "You're nothing but a pack of cards!"

Suddenly the whole pack rose up into the air and came flying down upon her! She screamed, and tried to beat them off—

—then found herself lying on the bank, with her head in the lap of her sister, who was gently brushing away some dead leaves that had fluttered down from the trees onto Alice's face.

"Wake up, Alice dear!" said her sister. "What a long sleep you've had!"

"Oh, I've had such a curious dream!" said Alice. And she told her sister, as well as she could remember them, all these strange Adventures of hers that you have just been reading about.

ALICE'S ADVENTURES
IN WONDERLAND

When she had finished, her sister kissed her, and said, "That *was* a curious dream, dear. Now run in and have your tea. It's getting late."

So Alice got up and ran off, thinking while she ran what a wonderful dream it had been.

But her sister sat, leaning her head on her hand, watching the setting sun, and thinking of little Alice and all her Adventures. With closed eyes, she thought back on her own youth. She half believed that she herself was in Wonderland, a bright-eyed little child once again, filled with simple joys and the curious, wonderful dreams of happy summer days.

THE END

LEWIS CARROLL

Charles Lutwidge Dodgson (Lewis Carroll) was born in 1832, one of eleven children of a country parson. He was a very bright child and student, but he stuttered, and this bothered him all his life. He attended college at Oxford, went on to teach mathematics there, was ordained as a minister, and remained at Oxford the rest of his life.

Although he was snobbish, cranky, and stern, children liked him and he adored children. In 1862, he took several people, including three daughters of a college dean, out on a boat trip, where they were caught in a rainstorm. Later, Alice, the middle daughter, asked Dodgson to tell a story. He made up a funny tale about Alice and some animals in a pool of tears. He included everyone from the rained-out boat trip (sisters Lorina and Edith were the Lory and the Eaglet, Dodgson was the Dodo, a Mr. Duckworth was the Duck, etc.). This was the start of *Alice's Adventures in Wonderland*, which Dodgson published under the name of Lewis Carroll in 1865.

The book was a sensation. Lewis Carroll went on to publish *Through the Looking Glass* in 1871. He died in 1898. His books went on to change ideas about children's literature forever.